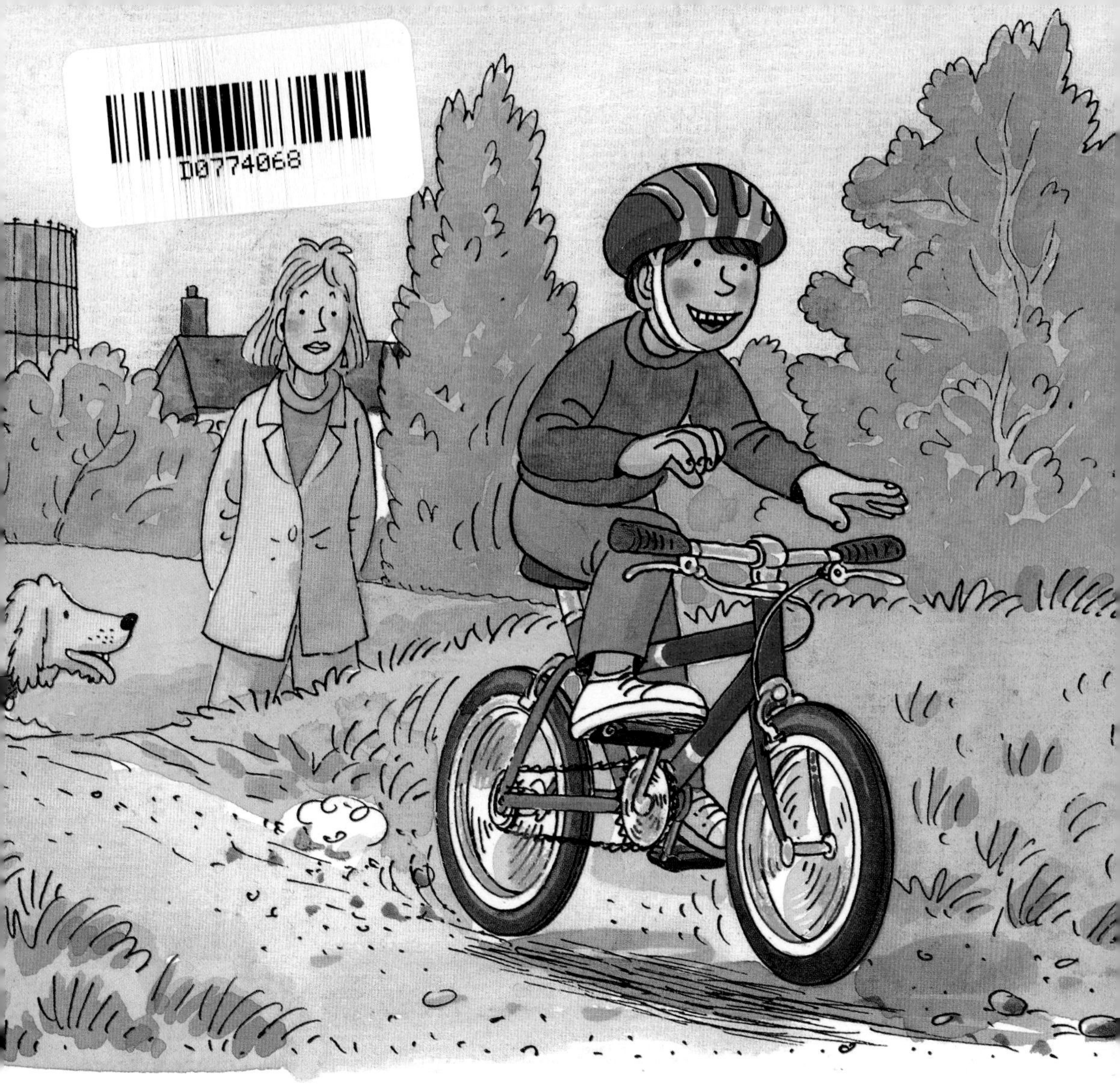

Look at me, Mum.

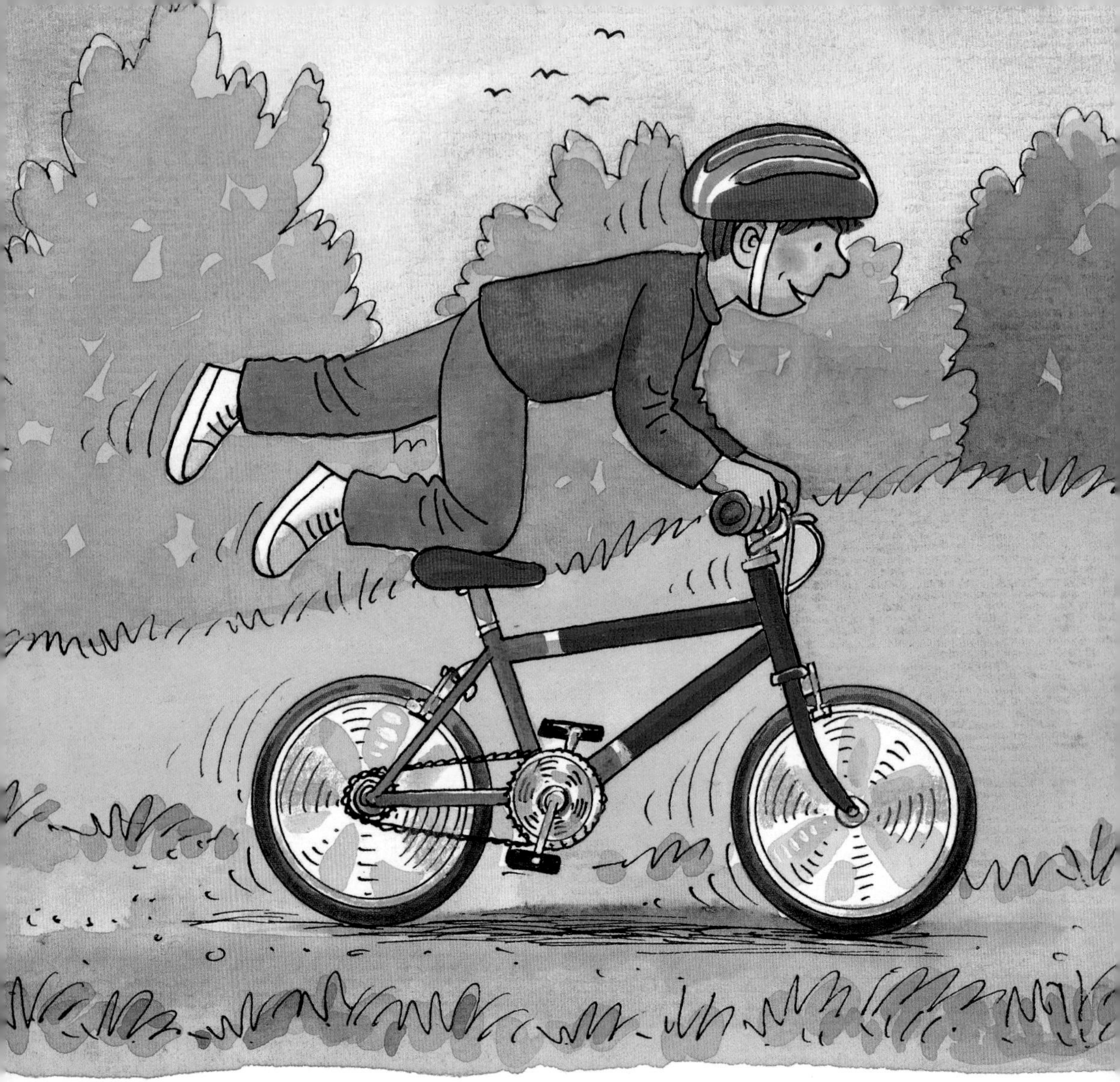

Look at me, Mum.

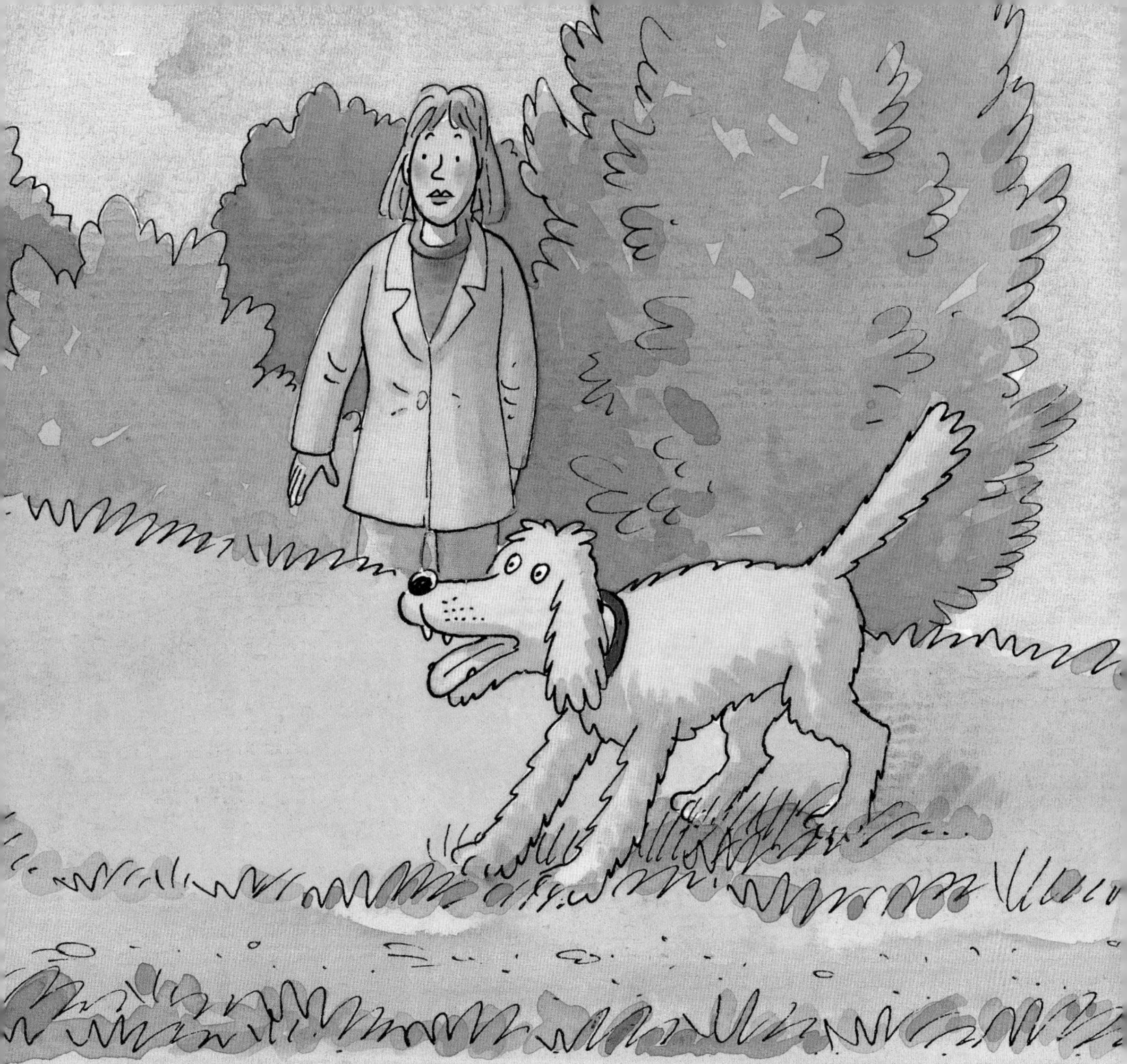

Look at me on my bike.

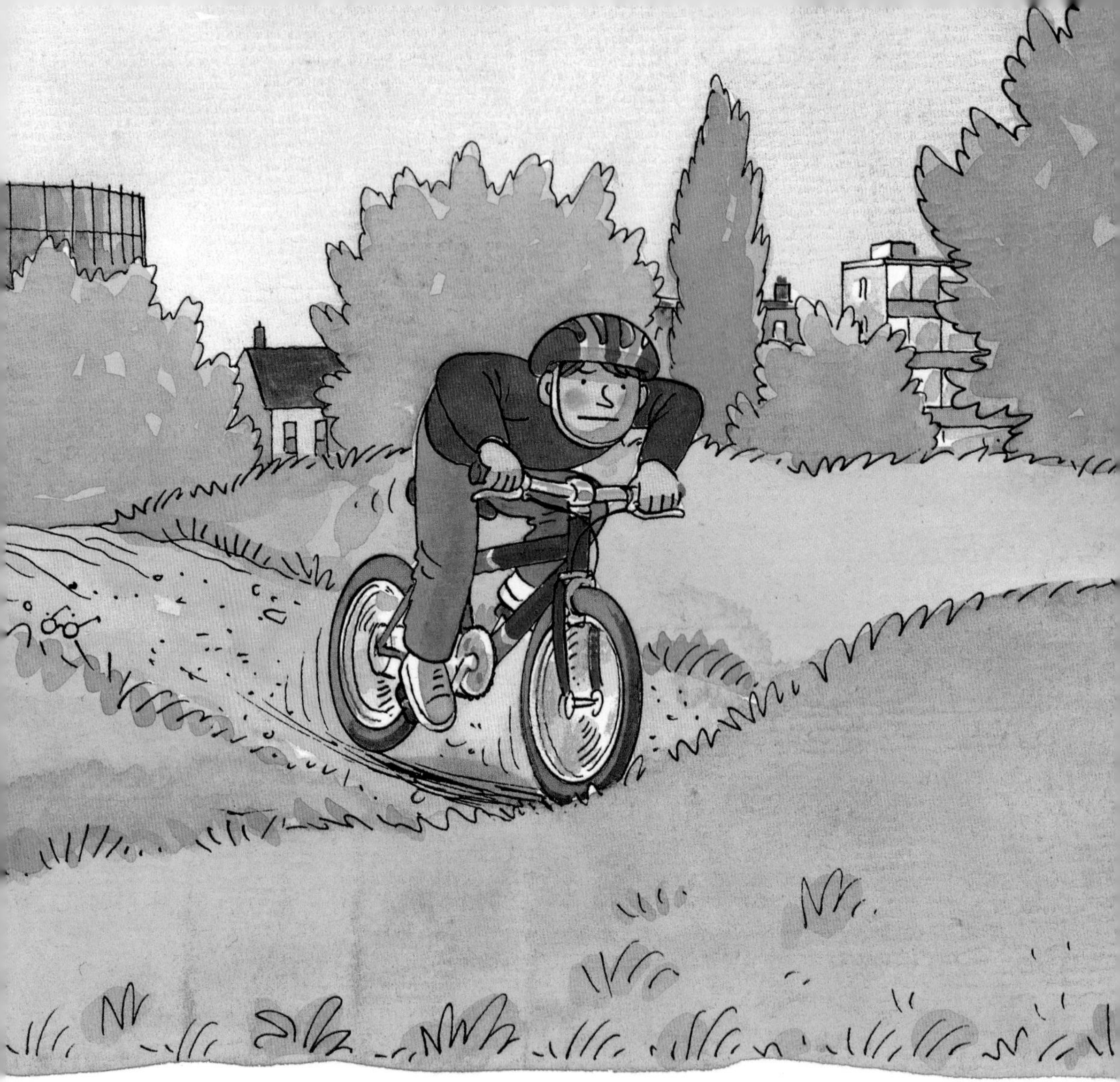

Look at me, Mum.

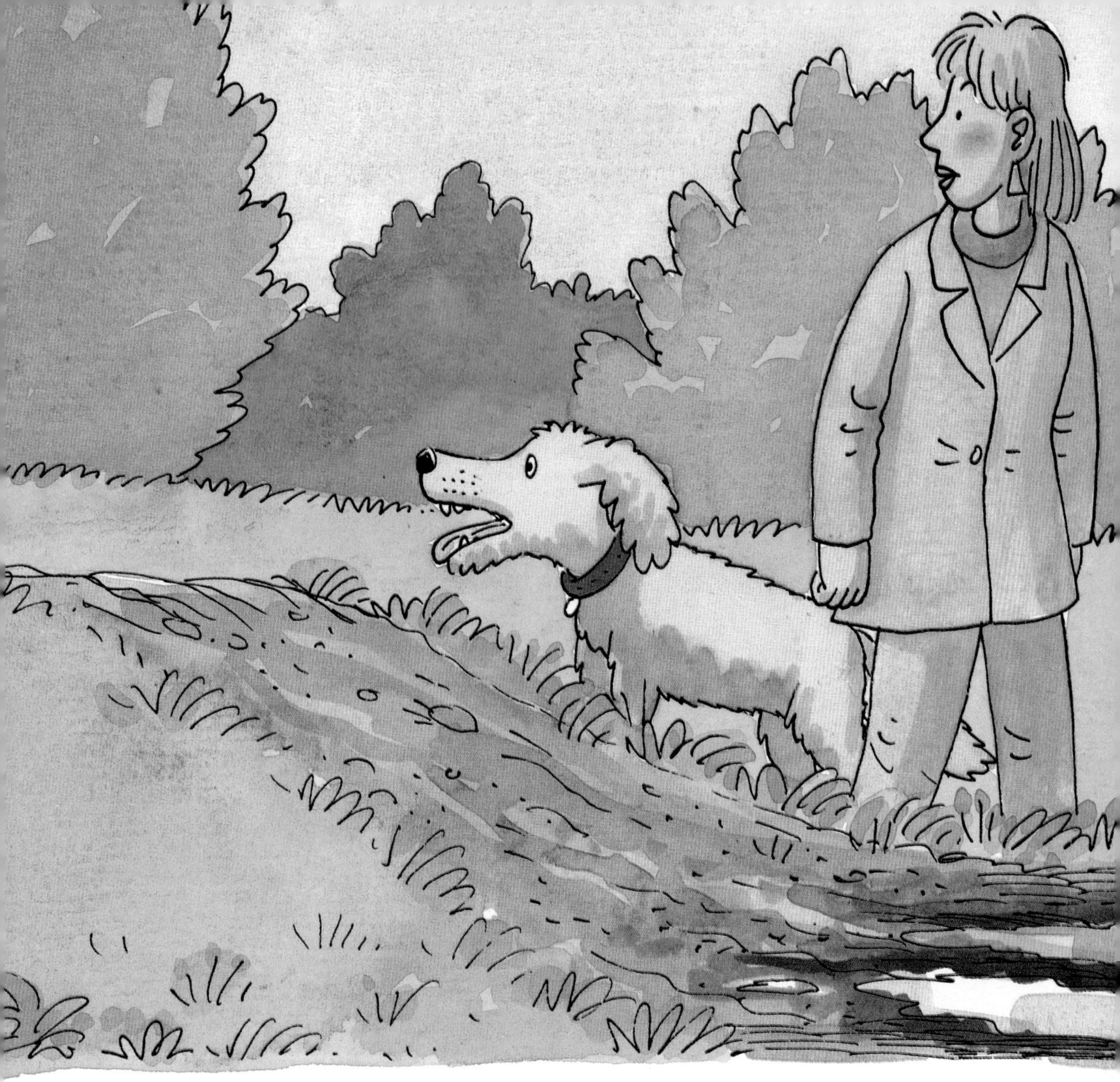

Look at me on my bike.

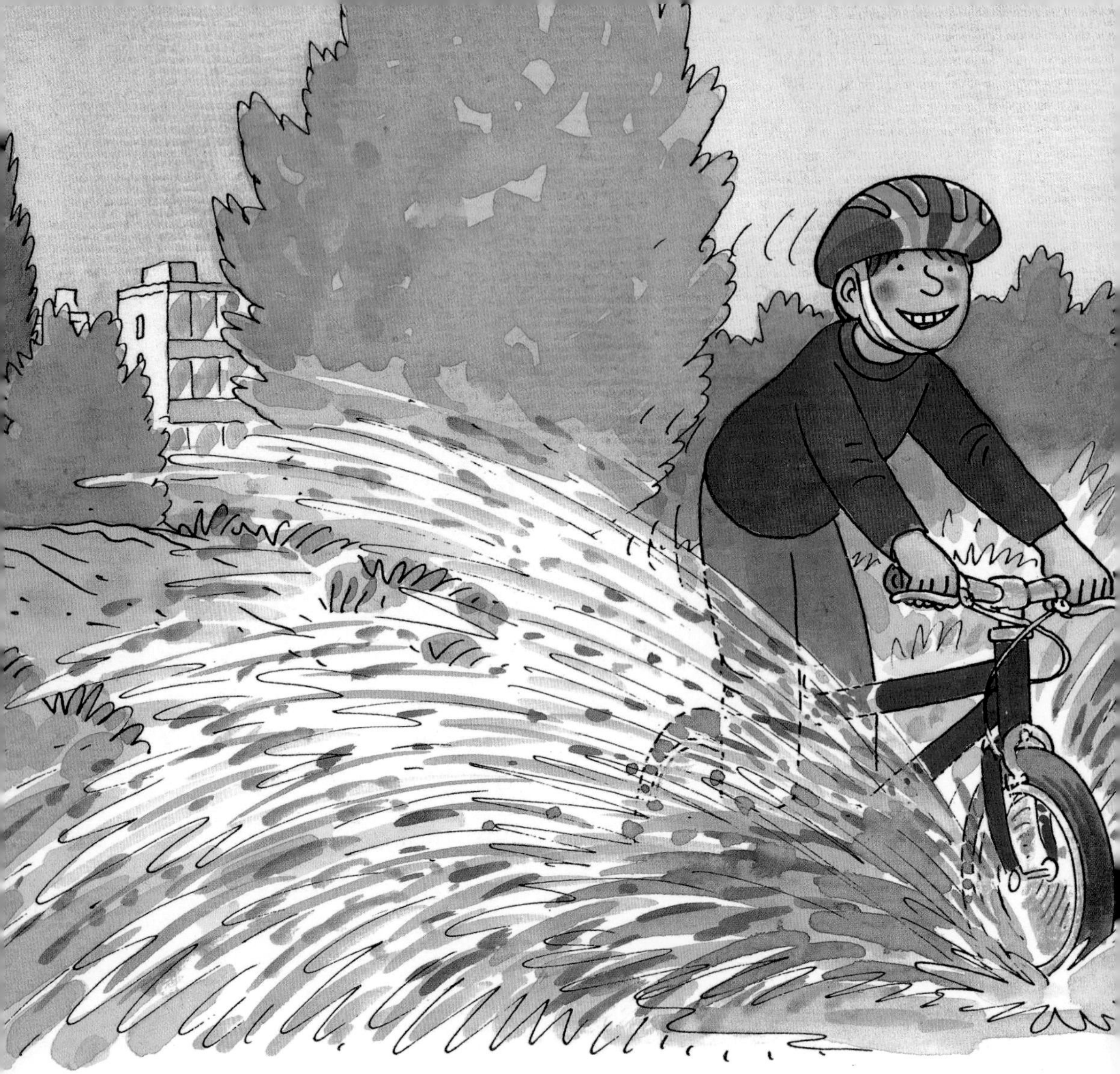

Look at me, Mum.

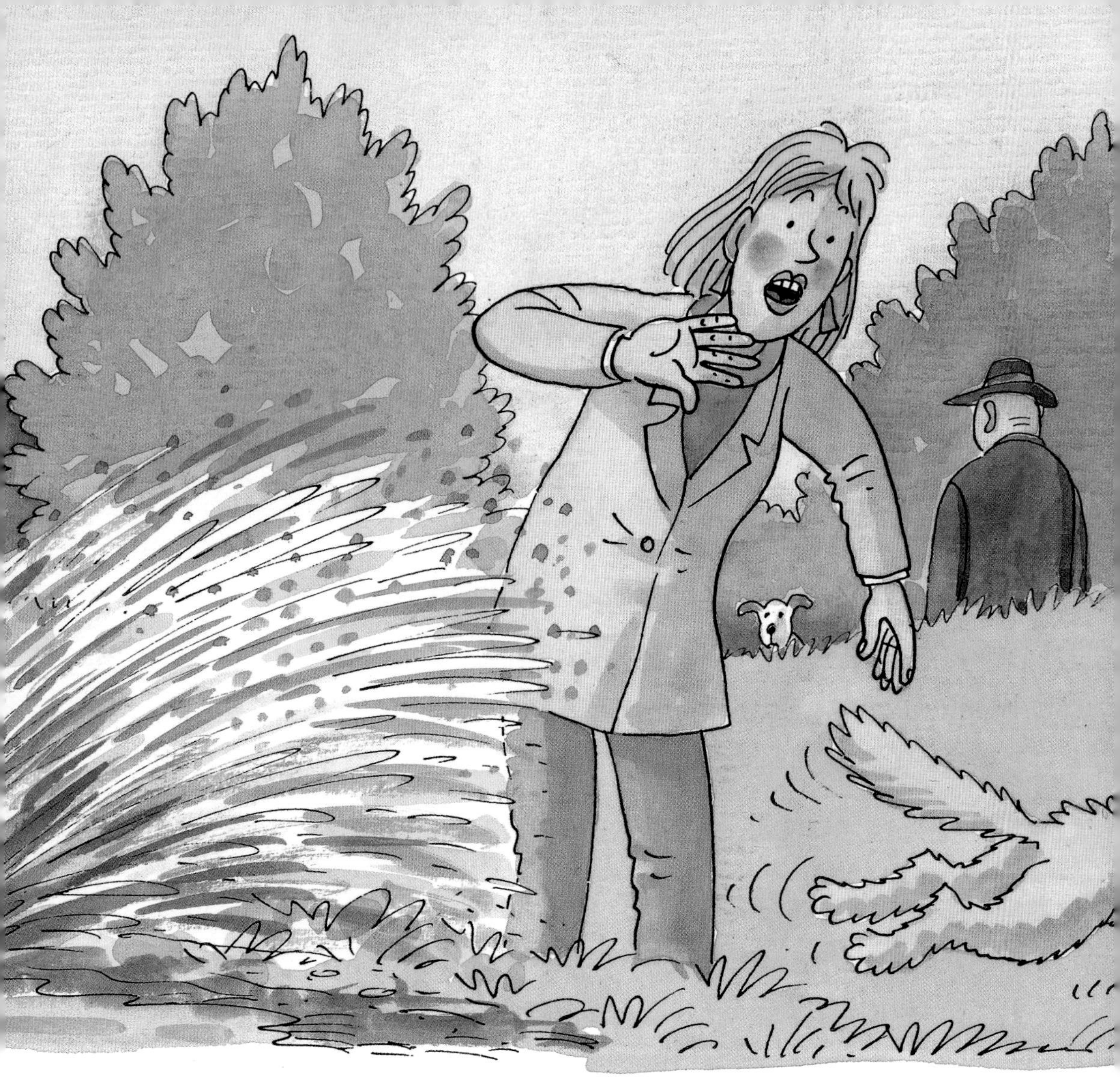

Oh, no!

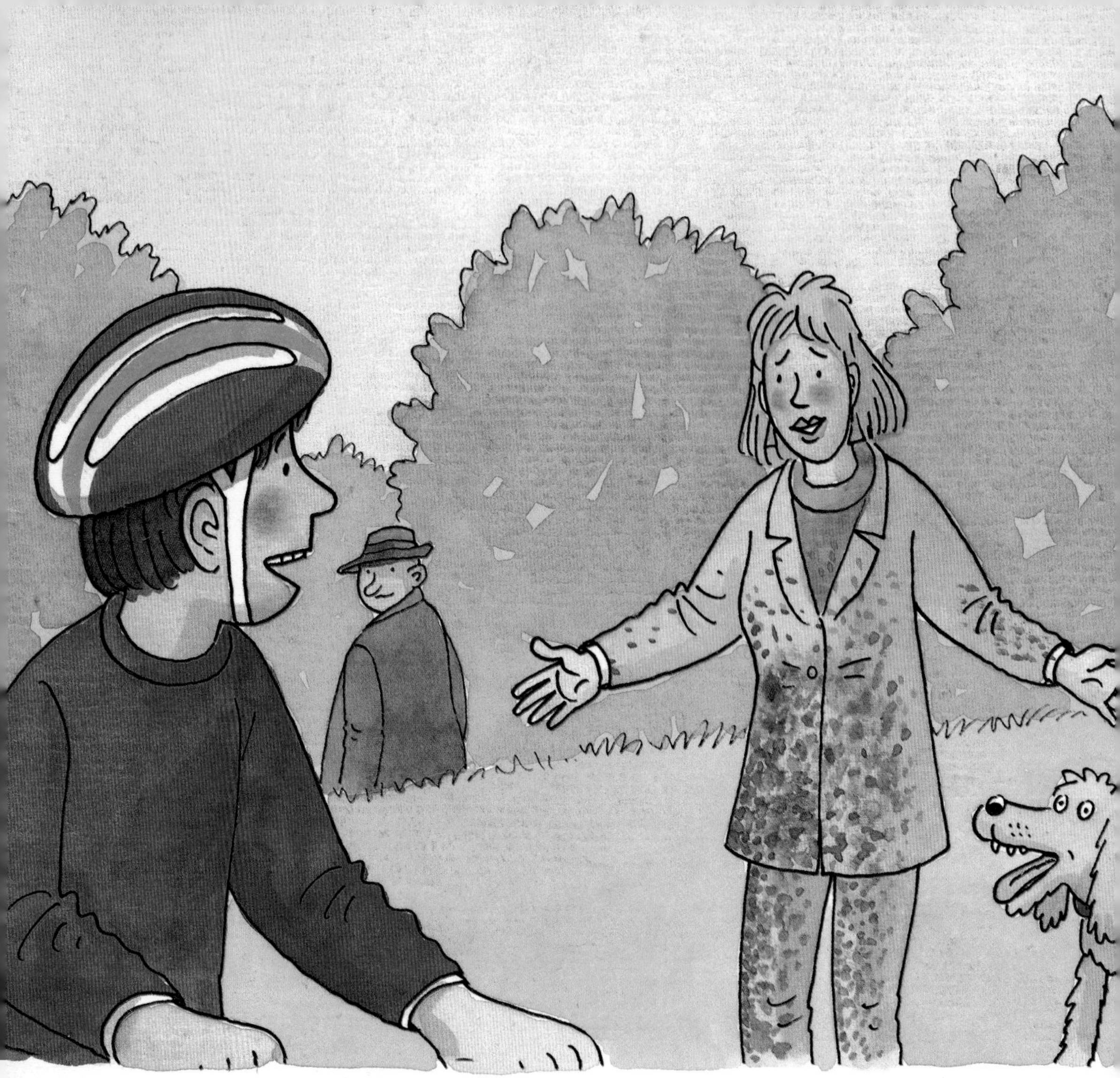

Look at me!